The Swan's Stories

"*I've seen and heard some peculiar things on my travels.*"

The Swan's Stories

HANS CHRISTIAN ANDERSEN

SELECTED AND TRANSLATED BY

BRIAN ALDERSON

ILLUSTRATED BY

CHRIS RIDDELL

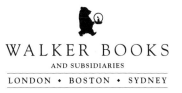

WALKER BOOKS
AND SUBSIDIARIES
LONDON • BOSTON • SYDNEY

First published 1997 by Walker Books Ltd
87 Vauxhall Walk, London SE11 5HJ

10 9 8 7 6 5 4 3 2 1

Text © 1997 Brian Alderson
Illustrations © 1997 Chris Riddell

This book has been typeset in Bulmer.

Printed in Italy

British Library Cataloguing in Publication Data
A catalogue record for this book is available from the British Library.

ISBN 0-7445-3298-1

FOR FRITZ ❦ B.A.

FOR JACK ❦ C.R.

*S*ometimes too, he would peer down into the bedrooms

and the children's nurseries.

THE STORY OF THE STORIES

*O*nce upon a time, before people invented comfy things like motor cars and TV sets, there was, living in Denmark, an old swan. He hadn't always been an old swan; in fact he had once been a very young swan – so young and frizzy and gawky, that people thought he wasn't a swan at all, but a duckling, – and not a very handsome duckling at that.

But a swan he was, and – as it turned out – a very inquisitive one. He went everywhere. He plodded round the yards and the lanes and the cobbled streets, poking his beak into people's doors and windows. He flew round the barns and the house-tops. Sometimes too, he would perch in the gutters and peer down into the bedrooms and the children's nurseries. Everything then looked upside-down, but that's not unusual. We all spend plenty of time seeing things the wrong way round.

After many years of looking at the antics of those around him, the swan decided that he ought to set down some of his experiences. "They may not be very instructive," he said, "and I'm afraid that they may not have a moral; but I've seen and heard some peculiar things on my travels, and folk might like to know about them. Everyone likes to hear what's going on in the house next door."

So the swan flew over to the duck-pond, and there he found an old newt sitting on a stone in the sunshine. He had a goose quill in his long, knobby fingers, a pot of Stephens's waterproof ink at his feet and a lily pad on his knee, for he was a literary newt and he was trying to write a poem. "Ahem!" said the swan. "I am sorry to trouble you, but I am eager to give the world my experiences, but –" waving a webby foot – "I need an amanuensis."

"Say on, friend," said the newt, for he was having difficulty with rhymes and was glad to be interrupted. So the swan began to dictate and the newt diligently wrote everything down on the pad of lily pads.

Fortunately for us, the pad was later picked up by a learned mole who put it in his book collection, and he has allowed us to print here some of the stories which the old swan told about the things he'd seen.

He wasn't really a swan, you know. Sometimes perhaps he thought he was - telling that tale, which so many people have heard, about an ugly duckling, suffering all winter long and then growing into a big, glorious bird. It seemed so like his own life, for he was born poor and brought up hard. Everyone laughed at him for being a great gawky fellow; but somehow he knew that some kind of swan-dom was out there waiting for him, and he just plodded on till he got to it.

Everyone knows him now for his stories – all round the world – but it wasn't like that when he set out. "The theatre": that was the thing. Perhaps he'd be an actor, or a playwright – and after he'd left home and gone to live near the lords and ladies of the capital city he even became a dancer. Huh! some dancer too, the great gawky fellow.

But he did write plays, and he wrote novels, and he wrote poetry. People were impressed. But the acting and the writing suddenly came together in a way that he hadn't bargained for and he started to make up stories to tell to children:

"A soldier came marching along the road: one, two! one, two! He had his knapsack on his back and his sword by his side – for he'd been at the war and now he was off home…"

Those are the first words of the first story that he had printed, the tale of a soldier and a magic tinder-box; and as time went by, other stories of high magic and fantastic events were to follow – one of them perhaps the most marvellous story ever told to children: the tale of the Snow Queen.

Wonder-tales like that were not everything though. Like the Browney at the grocer's, he knew that people needed porridge alongside poetry, and he looked at the world with a beady eye. "There's nowt so queer as folk," he might have said if he'd lived in Doncaster instead of Denmark, and many of his stories have no real magic in them at all, but rather take a sideways comic look at the queerness of folk. (Even when there's a flying trunk, there's a story about boastful matches.)

For sure, nothing is altogether straightforward. You see, he never lost his liking for the theatre, and these stories about everyday life are often dressed up like little pantomimes. Sometimes, like the widow with the pug-dog, people are at the centre of the stage. Sometimes they hang around near the edges of the set, slicing fish or putting up Christmas decorations. More often though what comes alive and makes the pantomime worth watching is not people at all but a lot of pots and pans and toys, or just a darning-needle or a collar. Simple creatures these, lying around in attics and kitchens and living-rooms, but Hans Christian Andersen saw them, and – more than that – he saw *into* them. "Why now," he might have said, "that's just like folk. I reckon there's a story in that. Let's see how it goes…"

Brian Alderson

10

LIST OF CONTENTS AND COLOUR PICTURES

Frontispiece

*"I've seen and heard some peculiar
things on my travels."*

The Story of the Stories....7

*Sometimes too, he would peer down
into the bedrooms and the children's
nurseries....6*

The Flying Trunk....13

*And so he arrived in Turkey....15
Good Lord! How the matches
sputtered and flamed!....23*

The Steadfast Tin-soldier....27

*"Tin-soldier!" said the goblin. "You
keep your eyes to yourself."....31
The cook seized the soldier round his
middle with two fingers....35*

The Money-pig....39

*The money-pig was thrilled
in his own way....42*

Jumpers....47

*"The highest jump is the jump up to
my daughter," said the king. "You
can't go higher than that."....50*

Lovers....53

*The top watched as the ball flew up
in the air like a bird....55*

The Collar....61

*The smoothing-iron imagined
that she was a steam-engine on
the railway....63*

The Darning-needle....69

*"Now I'm a brooch," said the darning-
needle. "I always knew I was bound
for higher things."....71
And so she sat there stiffly and
thought many thoughts....75*

Grief....79

*Every time the gate opened she
looked for as long as she could....82*

**The Shepherdess and the
Chimney-sweep....85**

*He was always looking at the table
under the mirror....87
"Now the old Chinaman's coming!"
screamed the little shepherdess....91
The old Chinaman had fallen
down off the table....95*

The Browney at the Grocer's....99

*Never had the little browney
imagined such glory....103
The greatest treasure in the house
was saved!....106*

The Snowman....109

*"You're stupid," said the watchdog,
"but then you've only just been
slapped together."....111
"I was young once," said the watchdog.
"And I lay in a velvet chair."....115
It was a long, long night – but
not for the snowman....119*

The Fir Tree....123

*"Where are they taken to?" asked
the fir tree....127
They hung little nets cut from coloured
paper and every net was filled
with sweets....131
The tree stood quiet and thoughtful
the whole night long....135*

∞

Some Words from the Mole....142
Acknowledgements....144

The Flying Trunk

ONCE UPON A TIME there was a merchant, and he was so rich that he could have paved the whole street with silver shillings, and the next little alleyway, too. But he didn't actually do that because he knew of a different way to use his money. If he spent a shilling of it then he got back half a crown – that's the sort of merchant he was. And then he died.

His son now got all this money and he had a fine old time with it. He went out to fancy-dress dances every night, made paper kites from five-pound notes, and played ducks-and-drakes with gold pieces instead of stones. "That's the way the money goes," they say – and that's the way it went, so that eventually he'd no more than four shillings, and no clothes except for a pair of slippers and an old dressing-gown. His friends didn't bother about him any more now, since they couldn't walk down the street with him, but one of them, who was a kind fellow, sent him an old trunk and said: "Pack up!" Oh, yes – that really was very kind, but he didn't have anything that he *could* pack up, so he got into the trunk himself.

It was a magic trunk. As soon as you twiddled the lock, the trunk could take off into the air, and that's what it did now – whoops! – up the chimney, high over the clouds, farther and farther away. The bottom of the trunk kept creaking and he was scared that it would fall apart – then he'd have done a very funny somersault! – "Lord preserve us!" – and so he arrived in Turkey. He hid the trunk in a wood under some dry leaves and set off for the town – and that was all right because all the Turks went around just like him in dressing-gowns and slippers. Then he met a nurse with a little baby: "Here, Turkish nurse," says he, "what's that big palace over there by the town, with all those high windows?"

"That's where the king's daughter lives," said the nurse. "There's a prophecy that she's going to be unlucky in love, so no one's allowed near her unless the king and queen are there."

And so he arrived in Turkey.

"Thanks," said the merchant's son, and he went back to the wood, sat in his trunk, flew up to the roof and crept in at the princess's window.

She was lying on her sofa asleep, and she was so beautiful that the merchant's son couldn't stop himself kissing her. So she woke up and was absolutely terrified, but he told her that he was one of the Turkish gods, who had flown down to her through the skies, and that cheered her up.

They sat together side by side and he told her stories about her eyes – that they were the most beautiful dark lakes, with thoughts swimming about in them like mermaids; and he told her about the storks, who bring little babies.

Oh, yes, they were altogether charming stories; so he asked the princess to marry him, and she said "Yes" straight away.

"But you must come back on Saturday," she said. "That's when the king and queen come round to tea. They'll be very proud that I'm going to marry a Turkish god, but just you see that you have a really nice fairy tale ready, because that's what my parents like best of all. My mother likes them to be very proper, with a moral, and my father likes them funny, so that you can laugh!"

"Right ho! I won't bring any wedding present except a story," says he, and so they parted, but the princess gave him a scimitar, inlaid with gold pieces, and that was a lot of use I must say.

He flew off, bought himself a new dressing-gown, and sat outside in the wood making up a fairy tale; it had to be finished by Saturday and that's not always so easy.

But then it was finished, and that was Saturday.

The king, the queen and the whole court came along for tea at the princess's. He was received most graciously.

"Will you tell us a fairy tale, then?" said the queen, "one that is profound and edifying?"

"But one we can laugh at," said the king.

"Right ho!" he said and he told it.

Now you listen to it carefully:

17

Once upon a time there was a bundle of matches who were inordinately proud, and that was because of their noble ancestry. Their family tree – that is to say the big fir tree out of which each of them was a little chip – had been a huge old tree in the forest. These matches now lay on the shelf between the tinder-box and an old iron pot and they were telling them about the days of their youth.

"Yes," they said, "when we were up on top of the tree, then we really were at the top of the tree! Morning and evening: diamond-tea (that was the dew); sunshine all day long (when the sun was shining) and all the little birds telling us stories. We could see very well how rich we were, because the other trees only got dressed in summer, while our family were able to dress in green summer and winter alike. But then came the woodcutter – that is to say the Great Revolution – and we were all split up. The head of the family got a position as main-mast in a splendid ship that could sail round the world if it wanted to; other branches went elsewhere, and we now have the task of spreading light among the lower orders – that's what respectable people like ourselves are doing down here in the kitchen."

"Well now, I've had a quite different run of fortune," said the iron pot that stood beside the matches. "Ever since I came into the world – time and time again – I've been scoured and cooked in. My job's to do with solid realities and I'm surely reckoned the foremost person in the house. My only pleasure is lying clean and neat here on the shelf after supper and carrying out a learned conversation with my colleagues; but, while I except the bucket, who sometimes gets taken down to the courtyard, we do always live indoors. Our only source of news is the shopping basket, but she chatters very irresponsibly about the government and the people; indeed, the other day she frightened an old pot so much that he fell down and smashed himself to smithereens! If you ask me, she's one of those militants!"

"Now you're jabbering too much!" said the tinder-box, and his steel banged against his flints so that sparks flew out. "Why don't we have a jolly evening?"

"Yes, let's talk about which of us is the most respectable," said the matches.

"No, I don't want to talk about myself," said an earthern pot. "Let's have a discussion evening. I'll begin. I'll tell you about something that everyone knows about, then you can all see yourselves as part of it and enjoy it.

On the Baltic, beside the Danish beech-trees…"

"What a beautiful beginning!" said all the
dishes. "This is bound to be a story we shall like!"

"Yes – I passed my youth there, in a quiet household. The furniture was polished, the floor scoured,
and new curtains every fortnight!"

"What an interesting way to tell a story," said
a carpet-sweeper. "You can hear straight away that
it's somebody feminine who's telling it; there's
something so pure and clean about it all!"

"Yes, one does feel that," said the bucket,
and she gave a little hop for joy, so that
she went clang on the floor.

And the pot continued her tale
and the end was just as good
as the beginning.

All the dishes
clattered for joy and the
carpet-sweeper took some green
parsley out of her dust-box and
decorated the pot, because she knew it
would make the others cross,
and, if I decorate her today,
she thought, then she'll
decorate me tomorrow.

"Now I'm going to dance!" said the fire-tongs, and
she danced. Good Lord! How she could do high kicks on
one leg! The old armchair cushion burst his seams just
looking at it!

"Perhaps I'll get a decoration too," said the
fire-tongs, and she did get one.

But they're only common people, thought
the matches.

Now it was the tea-urn's turn to sing, but she
said she'd got a cold and couldn't sing anyway unless
she got to boiling-point – but that was just her
affectation. Really, she wasn't going to sing unless she
was on the table in the best parlour.

Up in the window sat an old quill-pen which the
housemaid used for writing. There was nothing at all
remarkable about her except that she'd been dipped
too deep in the ink-well, but she was rather proud
of that. "If the tea-urn won't sing," she said, "she
needn't bother! There's a nightingale in a cage out
there and he can sing. He's never had a proper educa-
tion – but we won't be rude about that this evening."

"I find it highly unsuitable," said the tea-kettle,
who was the leading singer in the kitchen, and
half-sister to the tea-urn, "that we should listen
to a foreign bird like that. Is such a thing patriotic?

21

I will ask the shopping basket to decide."

"I am very cross!" said the shopping basket.
"You can't imagine how deeply cross I am. Is this a
suitable way to spend an evening? Wouldn't it be
better to put the house in order? Everyone should go
to his own place and I will manage the whole affair.
That will really be something!"

"Yes, let's have a rumpus!" they all said together –
but at the self-same moment the door opened. It was
the housemaid, and they all stood still; nobody spoke
a word. But there wasn't a pot there who didn't
know what she could really do, and how very
respectable she was. Oh, yes, they all thought, if I'd
wanted to, I could have made that a pretty jolly
evening!

The housemaid took the matches and lit the
fire with them – Good Lord! How they sputtered and
flamed!

Now, they thought, everyone can see that
we are the best! How bright we are! How we shine!

And then they burnt out…

"That was a beautiful story," said the queen.
"I really felt that I was there in the kitchen with the
matches; yes, now you may have our daughter."

*Good Lord! How the matches
sputtered and flamed!*

"Yes, indeed," said the king, "you may marry our daughter on Monday." And they talked to him like a son, because now he was one of the family.

The wedding was fixed, and the evening before it the whole town was illuminated. Cakes and buns were tossed out for grabs; the street urchins stood on their toes, shouted "Hurrah!" and whistled through their fingers. It was uncommonly splendid.

Ah, yes, I must see if I can do something too, thought the merchant's son, and so he bought some rockets and some crackers and all the fireworks he could think of, put them in his trunk and flew up in the air with them.

Whoosh! How they went! How they exploded!

All the Turks hopped up and down so that their slippers flew round their ears – they'd never seen signs and portents like that in the sky before. Now they knew that it really was a Turkish god who was going to marry the princess.

As soon as the merchant's son got back to the wood with his trunk, he thought, I'll just go back into the town again to see if I can hear how everybody liked it. And, of course, it was quite understandable that he'd want to do that.

No – but everyone was talking about it! Every single person he asked had seen it a different way, but everybody was absolutely delighted with it.

"I myself saw the Turkish god," said one. "He has eyes like glittering stars and a beard like foaming water!"

"He flew in a cloak of flame," said another, "with the prettiest little cherub peeping out of the folds."

Yes, they were marvellous things he heard – and the next day was going to be his wedding day.

Now he went back to the wood to have a rest in his trunk – but where was it? The trunk was all burnt up. A spark from those fireworks had been left behind, had caught fire, and the trunk was in ashes. He could no longer fly, no longer come to his bride.

She stood on the roof for the whole day, waiting. She's still waiting.

But he goes round the world telling stories – never a one, though, so jolly as the one about the matches.

∞

The Steadfast Tin-soldier

ONCE UPON A TIME there were twenty-five tin-soldiers – all brothers because they were made from one old tin spoon. They shouldered their muskets, eyes to the front, very handsome in their blue and black uniforms. The first thing they heard in all the world, when the lid was taken off the box where they lay, was the word "Tin-soldiers!" It was shouted by a little boy, who clapped his hands, for he'd been given them for his birthday, and now he stood them up on the table. Each soldier was exactly like the rest, except for one who was a bit odd: he'd only got one leg because he'd been made last and there hadn't been enough tin to go round. Even so, he stood just as firm on his one leg as the others did on their two, and he's the one who turns out to be worth talking about.

On the table, where they'd been stood up, there were lots of other toys, but the one that really caught your eye was a beautiful paper castle. You could see right into the rooms through the tiny windows, while outside tiny trees stood round a little mirror that was meant to be a lake. Swans made of wax were swimming on it and were reflected in it. It really was absolutely beautiful – but the most beautiful thing of all was a little lady who stood right in the open door of the castle. She too had been cut out of paper, but she had a skirt on, made of the finest muslin, and a narrow little blue ribbon over her shoulder like a sash – and in the middle of this there was a glittering tinsel star as big as her head. The little lady stretched out both her arms, for she was a dancer, and she lifted one leg so high in the air that the tin-soldier couldn't see where it was, so he thought that she'd only got one leg, just like him.

That would be the wife for me, he thought, but she's very grand. She lives there in that castle while I've only got a box – and there are twenty-five of us in that so there's not much room for her! Still – we must try to get acquainted. And so he lay down full length behind a snuff-box which stood on the table. Here he could easily watch the dainty little lady who went on standing on one leg without losing her balance.

When evening came, all the other tin-soldiers returned to their box and the people of the house went to bed. Now the toys began to play games: "visiting", "little wars" and "holding a dance". The tin-soldiers rattled about in their box, because they wanted to join in, but they couldn't get the lid off. The nutcrackers turned somersaults and the slate-pencil played games on the slate. There was such a to-do that the canary woke up and began to talk as well – and he spoke in verse. The only two who never moved from their places were the tin-soldier and the little dancer. She held herself so straight on the tip of her toe, with both arms outstretched, and he was just as steadfast on his single leg. Never for a moment did he stop looking at her.

Now the clock struck twelve and – whisk! – the lid sprang up from the snuff-box; but there was no tobacco in it, oh, no, just a little black goblin, for you see it was a trick snuff-box.

"Tin-soldier!" said the goblin. "You keep your eyes to yourself."

But the tin-soldier pretended that he hadn't heard him.

"All right – you wait till tomorrow," said the goblin.

So when it was morning and the children got up, the tin-soldier was stood up in the window and either it was the goblin or the draught that did it but the window suddenly flew open and the soldier fell head-over-heels from the third floor. That was a terrible journey – his leg stuck straight up in the air and he finished up on his helmet with his bayonet caught between the paving-stones.

The servant-girl and the little boy came down straight away to look for him, but although they almost trod on him they couldn't see him. If the tin-soldier had called out, "Here I am!" then they might have found him, but he didn't consider it proper to yell like that because he was in uniform.

Now it began to rain. The drops fell thicker and faster till it was a real storm, and when it was over two street-urchins came along.

"Hey, look!" said one of them. "There's a tin-soldier. Let's sail him!"

"*Tin-soldier!*" said the goblin.
"*You keep your eyes to yourself.*"

So they made a boat out of a newspaper, put the tin-soldier in, and he sailed off down the gutter. The two boys ran beside him clapping their hands. Lord preserve us! What waves there were in the gutter and what a flood it was – but then it really had been pouring with rain. The paper boat plunged up and down and now and then spun round so quickly that the tin-soldier was dizzy; but he stayed steady, never flinched, and went on shouldering his musket, eyes to the front.

All at once the boat floated into a long gutter-pipe – as dark as if he were back in his box.

Where am I coming to now? he thought. Oh, yes, this is all the goblin's fault! Ah, but if the little lady were here in the boat I wouldn't care if it were twice as dark!

Just then a big water-rat came along who lived in the gutter-pipe.

"Got a passport?" asked the rat. "Let's have your passport."

But the tin-soldier kept quiet and held his musket tighter than ever. The boat shot past with the rat after it. Hoo! how he snapped with his teeth and shouted out to bits of straw and wood: "Stop him! Stop him! He's not paid the toll! He's not shown his passport!"

But the current got stronger and stronger. The tin-soldier could already spy daylight where the pipe ended, but he also heard a roaring noise which might well have terrified a braver man than he was. Just you think about it – there, where the pipe ended, the gutter gushed out into a big canal and that was as dangerous for him as sailing over a waterfall would be for us.

By now he was so near it that he couldn't stop. The boat sped out and the poor tin-soldier held himself as upright as he could – no one should say of him that he even blinked his eyes. The boat whirled round three ... four times and then filled up to the brim with water – so it had to sink. The tin-soldier stood up to his neck in water and the boat sank deeper and deeper, the paper fell apart more and more, and the water came over the soldier's head – now he thought of the pretty little dancer that he'd never see again, and there sounded in the tin-soldier's ears the old song:

33

Onward, onward, warrior-man,
      The time has come to die!

And the paper parted and the tin-soldier fell through – but at that moment he was swallowed by a great big fish.

My word – but it was dark in there! It was even worse than in the gutter-pipe, and it was also very tight – but the tin-soldier was steadfast and lay there full-length, with his musket on his shoulder.

The fish jumped about, making the most amazing twists and turns, till at last he was still and something flashed through him like lightning. Daylight shone clear, and someone cried out loud:

"A tin-soldier!" The fish had been caught, taken to market, sold and brought up to the kitchen where the cook cut him open with a large knife. She seized the soldier round his middle with two fingers and carried him off to the room where everyone wanted to see this remarkable man who'd travelled about inside a fish – but the tin-soldier didn't let it go to his head. They stood him up on the table and there! – whoever would believe such wonders in the world! – the tin-soldier was in the self-same room that he'd been in before. He saw

The cook seized the soldier round his middle with two fingers.

the self-same boys, and the self-same playthings were on the table: the beautiful castle with the pretty little dancer. She still balanced herself on one leg and held the other high in the air, for she too was steadfast. That moved the tin-soldier. He almost wept tin tears, but that wouldn't have been proper. He looked at her, and she looked at him, but they never said a word.

Then all of a sudden one of the small boys took the soldier and threw him straight into the stove – without any reason whatsoever. No doubt the goblin in the snuff-box was really to blame.

The tin-soldier stood there, brilliantly lit, and felt a terrible burning – but he didn't know if that was because of the actual fire or because of his love. All his colours were gone, but no one could tell if that was because of his journeyings or because of his grief. He looked at the little lady. She looked at him and he felt himself melting, but he still stood there steadfast with his musket on his shoulder. Then the door opened. The draught picked up the dancer and she flew like a nymph of the air straight to the tin-soldier in the stove, burst into flames and was gone. Then the tin-soldier melted down into a lump and when the cook came

next day to take the ashes out she found him like a
little tin heart.

    All that was left of the dancer
    was the tinsel star and that was
    burnt black as a coal.

The Money-pig

THERE WERE SO MANY toys lying about in the children's room. Up over the cupboard stood an earthenware money-box in the shape of a pig, and of course it had a slit in its back and someone had scraped this slit bigger with a knife, so that you could fit large silver pieces in – what's more, two *had* been put in with a lot of smaller coins, as well. The money-pig was stuffed so full that he couldn't rattle any more, and that's the very best you can do if you're a money-pig. There he stood, up on the shelf, looking down at everything in the room and knowing very well that he could buy the whole lot with what he'd got in his stomach. When that happens, you come to have a high opinion of yourself. The others thought so too, and if they didn't say it that was because they had other things to think about.

A drawer in the chest was half-open and a big doll was sitting up there – rather old, with a rivet in her neck. She looked around and said, "Shall we play at 'People'? That's always fun." So a great rumpus started. Even the pictures turned round to the wall to show they'd got backs to them, but that wasn't because they were against the idea.

It was the middle of the night; the moon shone in through the window and lit the room up for nothing. So now the game could begin and everyone was invited to join in, even the go-kart, who really belonged with the rougher toys. "We're all worth something," he said. "We can't all be ladies and gents. Someone's got to make himself useful, as the saying goes."

The money-pig was the only one to get a written invitation. They thought he was too high up to hear if they called up to him, but he never said if he'd come, and he never came. If he was going to join in, he'd do it from home; they would have to look after things as well as they could, and that's what they did.

The little toy-theatre was set up so that he could see right inside. They wanted to begin with a comedy and then they'd have tea and an improving discussion – and they started with that straight away. The rocking-horse talked about training and bloodstock; the go-kart about railways and steam-engines – for these were things that were very much in their line of business and they could go on about them as long as you liked. The clock on the wall talked about the body politic – tick – tick – tick! He knew when the hour of destiny would strike, but they *said* he never told the right time.

The bamboo cane stood there, very proud of his brass bottom and his silver knob, nicely topped and tailed. On the sofa lay two embroidered cushions, pretty but stupid – and so the comedy could begin.

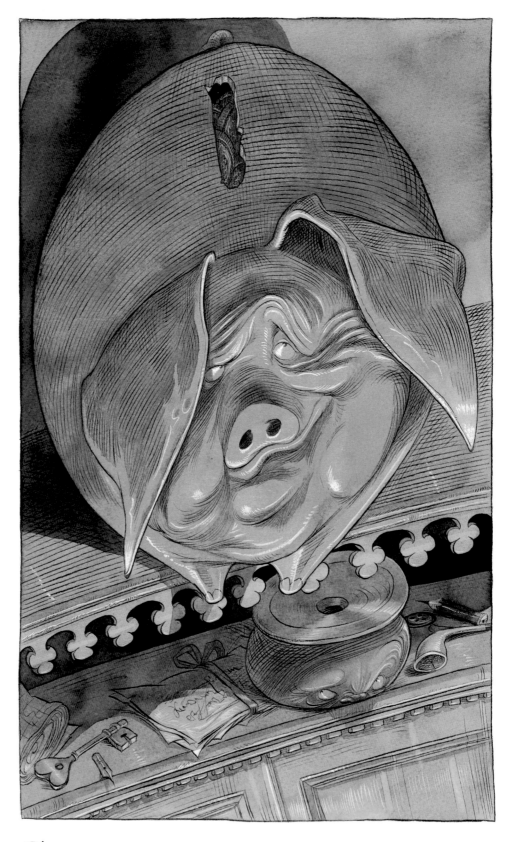

The money-pig was thrilled
in his own way.

Everybody sat there watching, and they were asked to clap, stamp and cheer just as if they were enjoying themselves. But the riding-whip said that he never clapped for the old folk, only for the ones not courting yet.

"I clap for everyone," said the cracker.

Everyone has his place, thought the spittoon, and that's what they all thought during the comedy. It wasn't much of a play, but they staged it well; all the actors turned their painted sides outwards, to be seen from the right direction and not from the wrong one, and all of them acted outstandingly, coming out past the footlights (their wires were too long, so that made them all the more remarkable). The doll was so thrilled that she snapped her rivet and the money-pig was so thrilled in his own way that he decided to do something for one or other of them, write them into his will so that whoever it was could be buried alongside him in the family vault when the time came.

It was all so enjoyable that they gave up the idea of having tea and stayed with the improving discussion – that's what they called playing "People" – all without any bad feeling at all – just playing; and each of them thought about himself and about what the money-pig might be thinking, and the money-pig thought most deeply of all, because he thought about Wills and Family Vaults, and when would be the time for such things...

Altogether sooner than expected.

CRASH!

Down he fell – down from the shelf – down on to the floor in smithereens, but the coins hopped and danced. The smallest ones spun like tops, the bigger ones rolled away – especially one of the big silver pieces, who set off on his own to see the world.

And that's what he came to, that's what they all came to, and the broken bits of the money-pig came to the dustbin.

But next day, up on the cupboard, there stood a new earthenware money-pig.

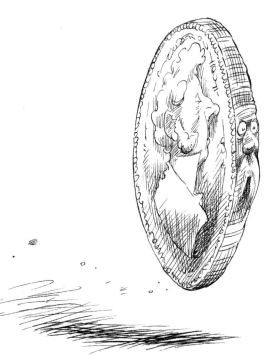

There weren't any
coins inside him, so he couldn't rattle – and to that
extent, he was just like the one before.

But he was only making a beginning –
so that's where we'll stop!

Jumpers

ONCE UPON A TIME, a flea, a grasshopper and a jumping-jack decided to see which of them could jump the highest. They invited the whole world to see the show, plus anyone else who wanted to come – so there the three great jumpers were, all together in the same room. "Right!" said the king. "I'll give my daughter to the one who can jump highest – for it's a poor do to have these chaps jumping for nothing."

The flea was the first to come forward. He had absolutely charming manners and bowed in all directions, for he had the blood of young ladies in his veins and he was quite used to going around in the company of people – and that counts for a lot.

Then came the grasshopper, who was certainly far heavier, but in pretty good shape. He was wearing the green uniform that he'd been born with. People said that he came of a very old family in the land of Egypt – much respected out there. He'd been brought in from the fields and put in a house of cards, which had three storeys to it, all built from court-cards with the coloured sides turned inwards; what's more, it had doors and windows cut out of the body of the Queen of Hearts. "I sing so beautifully," he said, "that sixteen crickets from these parts, who've been chirping ever since they were babies, but who've never had a house of cards, have got so envious listening to me that they've grown thinner than ever."

Both these two – the flea and the grasshopper – spoke up for themselves and made it pretty plain that they thought themselves well up to marrying a princess.

The jumping-jack never said a word, but people reckoned that that meant he was thinking all the more, and as soon as the court-dog had taken a sniff at him, he let it be known that the jumping-jack came from a good family. The old councillor, who'd had three medals for knowing when to hold his

tongue, assured everyone that he
could see that the jumping-jack had
the gift of prophecy. You could see from his
backbone if it was going to be a mild or a hard
winter – and that's not something you can see from
the backbone of the weatherman.

"Well, I'll not say more!" said the old king.
"I'll go on sitting here, thinking!"

Now the jumping began. The flea jumped so
high that no one could see where he went, so they
declared that he hadn't jumped at all – which was
very mean of them.

The grasshopper only jumped half as high, but
he jumped right into the king's face, who said
that was disgusting.

The jumping-jack stayed there,
quiet, for a long time – thinking.
People began to wonder if
he'd ever jump at all.

"I hope he's not been taken
ill," said the court-dog and sniffed
at him again, and – oops! – he
jumped a little sideways jump
into the lap of the princess, sitting
low down on her golden stool.

"*The highest jump is the jump up to my daughter,*"
said the king. "*You can't go higher than that.*"

Then the king said: "The highest jump is the jump up to my daughter, for you can't go higher than that – but you need brains to realize it and the jumping-jack's shown that he's got brains. Why – he thinks with his legs!"

And so the jumping-jack got the princess.

"But I jumped highest!" said the flea. "Still, it's always the same. Let her have her old wishbone with his twisted string and his bit of stick. I jumped highest; but in this world you need to build up your body if anyone's going to see you."

And so the flea went into the foreign legion where they say he got himself killed.

The grasshopper sat down outside in a ditch and thought about the way of the world and he said as well: "Body-build-ing is the thing. Body-building is the thing," and so he went on singing his monotonous song – which is where we picked up this story.

But some people think it's nothing but lies, even though it has been printed.

Lovers

A WHIPPING TOP AND A BALL were lying in a drawer along with some other playthings, and the whipping top said to the ball: "Why shouldn't we be lovers since we're both together in this drawer?" But the ball, whose cover was sewn from coloured morocco leather and who fancied herself as good as a fine lady, wouldn't even reply to such a thing.

The next day, the little boy who owned the toys came along. He painted the top in red and gold and banged a brass nail down his middle – it looked just splendid as the top whizzed round.

"Look at me!" he said to the ball. "What do you say now? Shouldn't we be lovers? We'd look so good together – you leaping and me dancing.

Nobody would be happier than us."

"That's what you think!" said the ball. "You still don't realize that my father and mother were a pair of morocco slippers and that I've got a cork inside me!"

"Well, all right – but I'm made of mahogany," said the top, "and the mayor himself turned me on his own lathe, and he was delighted with me."

"Oh, yes – and can I take your word for it?" asked the ball; and the top swore he might never be whipped again if he was telling fibs.

"You talk very nicely for someone like yourself," said the ball, "but I can't do anything; I'm as good as half engaged to a swallow. Every time I go up in the air, he sticks his head out of his nest and says 'Will 'oo? Will 'oo?', and now I've said to myself that I'll say 'yes', and that's as good as being half engaged. But I do promise I'll never forget you."

"Well, that's a big help," said the top; and that's all they said to each other.

Next day the ball was taken out. The top watched as it flew up in the air like a bird, so that in the end it was lost from sight. Every time it came back down again, every time, but it always gave a good bounce when it hit the ground (and that was either because of some inner yearning or because it

The top watched as the ball flew
up in the air like a bird.

had the cork inside it). But, the ninth time, the ball stayed gone and didn't come back down again, and the little boy looked for it and looked for it, but it just stayed gone.

"Well, I know where it is," sighed the top, "it's in the swallow's nest. She's got married to the swallow."

The more the top thought about it, the more he was taken with the ball. Just because he couldn't have her, he loved her the more – and the fact that she'd chosen someone else seemed peculiar to him; and the top danced, whizzing round, but always thinking of the ball – and in his thoughts she became prettier and prettier. And so, in that way, many years went by and she became an Old Love.

And the top was not young any more...! But one day he was covered all over in gilt. He'd never looked so handsome, for he was now a golden top, and he really jumped and whizzed – sheesh! That was something! But suddenly he jumped too high – and vanished.

They looked for him and looked for him, even down in the cellar, but he couldn't be found. Where on earth was he?

Well – he'd jumped into the dustbin where there were all kinds of things like cabbage-stalks, floor-sweepings and gravelly bits that had come down from the gutters.

"Now this is a nice place to be! My gilding won't last long here! What a rabble!" And he looked out of the corner of his eye at a long cabbage-stalk that was poked in all too near him, and at a strange round thing that looked like a rotten apple. But it wasn't an apple; it was an old ball that had lain up in the gutter for many years and was sodden with water.

"God be praised! Someone's come among us that a person can talk to," said the ball, considering the gilded top. "Do you know, I'm really made of morocco leather, sewn together by positively virginal hands – and I have a cork in my middle, though you wouldn't think so to look at me. I was going to be married to a swallow, but I fell into the gutter, and I've been lying there for five years, getting soaked. Believe me, that's a long time for a young girl!"

But the top didn't say anything. He thought about his old love, and the more he listened the clearer it was that this was she. Then the little servant-girl came along to turn out the rubbish. "Hey up! There's the golden top!" she said. And the top was brought back into the room with much praise and honour, but nothing more was heard of the ball. And the top never spoke again about his old affair.

Such things pass when your lover has lain five years in the gutter, soaking up water. Indeed, you don't really recognize her when you meet her in the dustbin.

The Collar

ONCE UPON A TIME there was
a splendid gentleman whose
worldly goods consisted of a
boot-jack and a comb, but he
had the most beautiful
collar in the world
and this story is
about that collar.
At the time we're
talking about he was
old enough to think
about marrying, and it so happened
that he met a lady's garter in the wash.

"Wow!" said the collar. "Never before have I
seen anything so slender and delicate, so sweet and
so pretty. May I ask your name?"

"I never tell anyone that," said the garter.

"Where do you live?" asked the collar.

But the garter was very shy and it seemed to her
that this was a very funny thing to be asked.

"You must be a girdle," said the collar, "a kind of under-girdle. I can see very well, my dear little lady, that you are both useful and decorative."

"You are not to talk to me!" said the garter. "I can't recall that I gave you permission to do so."

"Aha!" said the collar. "When anyone's as beautiful as you, then that's permission enough!"

"Don't you dare come so close!" said the garter. "You look to me to be too much like a man."

"Indeed, I am a splendid gentleman!" said the collar. "I've got a boot-jack and a comb!" (And that was not the truth, because it was his master who had them – he was just boasting.)

"Don't come near me!" said the garter. "I'm not used to it!"

"Hoity-toity!" said the collar; and then they were lifted out of the wash. They were starched, hung over a chair in the sunshine and then laid on the ironing board. Then along came the hot iron. "Madam!" said the collar. "Little widow-woman! I'm getting very hot! I'm getting to be a new man – losing my creases – oogh! You're burning a hole in me! Will you marry me?"

"Rag!" said the smoothing-iron, and she moved proudly over the collar, for she imagined that she was a steam-engine on the railway, pulling carriages.

The smoothing-iron imagined that she
was a steam-engine on the railway.

"Rag!" she said.

The collar was a little
bit frayed at the edges, so the
paper-scissors came to
trim the threads.

"Oh!" said
the collar, "You must be
a prima ballerina!
How you kick
your legs!
There's not a person
can do that like you!"

"I know," said the scissors.

"You deserve to be a countess!" said the collar.
"All I've got is a splendid gentleman, a boot-jack
and a comb! If only I were a count!"

"He's making a proposal!" said the scissors, and
she was so cross that she gave him a proper clip,
and he had to be retired.

"I'll have to propose to the comb," said
the collar. "It is remarkable how you
keep all your teeth, little lady!
Have you ever
thought of getting
engaged?"

"Yes, indeed, you ought to know that," said the comb. "I'm engaged to the boot-jack."

"Engaged!" said the collar.

Now there was no one left for him to propose to and so he took against the whole idea.

A long time went by, and then the collar found himself in a sack at the paper mill. That was a ragged bunch down there – but the fine ones kept to themselves, and the coarse ones kept to *them*selves, just as it ought to be. They all had a lot to tell, but the collar had the most because he was such a boastful fellow.

"I've had a fearful number of sweethearts!" said the collar. "I couldn't get away from them! Indeed, I was a splendid gentleman – very starchy! I had a boot-jack and a comb, and I never used either of them! You should have seen me a while back – seen me on my day off! I shall never forget my first sweetheart; she was a girdle – so delicate, so sweet and so pretty. She threw herself into a wash-tub for my sake! Later there was a widow-woman, really hot for me, but I let her wait and she turned quite black! Then there was a prima ballerina, and she gave me the scars I carry to this day; she was very bad-tempered! Even my own comb was in love with me, and lost all her teeth she was so love-sick. Oh, yes, I've endured many such blows; but I'm most sorry for the garter – I mean the girdle – who went in the wash-tub. I've got a lot on my conscience; I can't wait to be turned into white paper!"

And that's what happened. All the rags were turned into white paper, but the collar was turned into this very piece of white paper here in front of you with his story printed on it – and that's because he boasted so frightfully about things that weren't true.

And so we ought to watch out that we don't carry on in the same way, for we never know if we won't end up in a sack of rags and get turned into white paper and have our whole life-story printed on it – even the most secret bits. Then we'll find ourselves running around reciting it, just like the collar did.

∞

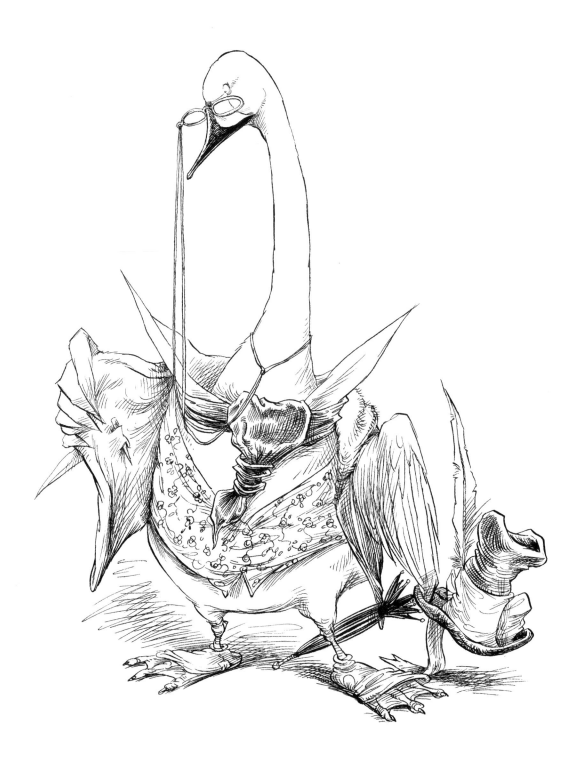

The Darning-needle

ONCE UPON A TIME there was a darning-needle who was so altogether fine that she fancied she was a sewing-needle.

"Mind how you hold me," said the darning-needle to the fingers that had picked her up. "Don't you drop me. I'm that fine that if ever I fall on the floor I'll never be found again."

"That's as may be," said the fingers, and they pinched her round her middle.

"Watch out! Here I come with my train!" said the darning-needle, and she drew a long thread after her – but it didn't have a knot at the end.

The fingers steered the needle towards the cook's slipper, where the upper leather had split and needed sewing together again.

"This is menial work," said the darning-needle. "I'll not go again. I'm breaking! I'm breaking!" And so she broke.

"Didn't I say so?" said the darning-needle. "I am too fine."

Now she's good for nothing, thought the fingers, but they still had to hold her tight while the cook dripped sealing-wax on to her and stuck her into the front of her apron.

"Just look – now I'm a brooch," said the darning-needle. "I always knew I was bound for higher things – if one is something then one will become something!" and she laughed to herself inside (for you can't see a darning-needle laughing from the outside); and there she sat, looking round on all sides, as proud as if she were driving along in a carriage.

"May I have the honour to enquire if you are gold?" she asked the pin, who was next to her. "You look very pretty, and you've got a head of your own, even if it is a little one. You must see if you can grow a bit, although it's not everyone who gets sealing-wax dropped on their end." And the darning-needle drew herself up so proudly that she fell out of the apron and into the sink just as the cook was rinsing it out.

"Now I'm a brooch," said the darning-needle.

"I always knew I was bound for higher things."

"Now we're going on our travels," said the darning-needle. "I hope I don't get lost." But she did.

"I am too fine for this world," she said, as she lay in the gutter, "but I have my good conscience and that's always a small comfort."

And the darning-needle held herself erect and never lost her composure.

All kinds of things sailed over her: sticks, straw, bits of old newspaper. "See how they sail along!" said the darning-needle. "None of them knows what's sticking up under them. I'm the one that's sticking up! I'm the one that's sitting here! Look now – there goes a stick, and it hasn't got a thought in the world except 'stick' – and that's just itself. There goes a straw: see how it swirls, see how it twirls! Don't you think about yourself so much or you'll run into the kerb! There goes a paper! Everything's forgotten that's been printed on it and yet it still thinks well of itself! Ah well, I sit here patiently and quietly. I know what I am and I'm staying that way!"

One day something came along beside her that shone so prettily the darning-needle thought it was a diamond – but it was a bit of broken bottle; and because it was shining, the darning-needle talked to it (giving herself out to be a brooch), "I suppose you're a diamond then?"

"Oh, yes, something like that!"

And so each one thought the other to be a person of quality, and they talked together about how conceited the world was.

"Oh, yes, I lived in a lady's box," said the darning-needle, "and the lady was a cook. She had five fingers on each hand, but I have never known anything so stuck-up as those five fingers, and yet they were only there to hold me – pick me out of the box, lay me back in the box!"

"Did they have brilliant connections?" asked the bit of bottle.

"Brilliant connections!" said the darning-needle. "Good heavens, no, but they were very conceited! They were five brothers all born 'Finger', and they all stuck by each other even though they were different sizes: the one at the end, Thumbkin, was short and fat. He was the one who went on the outside, so he had only one joint in his back and could only make a single bow, but he used to say that if he was chopped off a man, then that

meant the whole of the man was no good for fight-
ing in wars. Lickpot used to find his way into sweet
things and bitter things; he could point to the sun
and the moon, and he was the one who did the
work when they went in for writing. Long-man
looked out over the heads of the others. Goldie
went around with a gold ring round his tummy,
and Little Peter Playboy didn't do anything at all,
and was proud of the fact. They'd brag about this
and brag about that, so I cleared off down the
sink."

"And now we sit here winking," said the bit of
glass – and at that moment a lot more water gushed
down the gutter, so that it overflowed its banks and
the bit of glass was carried away.

"There! Now she's gone off to higher things,"
said the darning-needle, "but I stay sitting here.
I really am too fine, but I'm proud to be so and
that's a matter for respect." And so she sat there
stiffly and thought many thoughts.

"I could almost believe that I was born of a
sunbeam, I am so fine. Doesn't it seem that the
sunbeams are always seeking me out under the
water? Ah! I'm so fine that even my mother
wouldn't be able to find me! If I had my old eye,

*And so she sat there stiffly
and thought many thoughts.*

that broke off, I think I might even weep! No! Heaven forbid that I should – weeping is just not refined!"

One day a couple of street-urchins lay grubbing about in the gutter where they used to find old nails, pennies and suchlike things. It was pretty mucky but they enjoyed it very much.

"Ow!" said one of them – he'd pricked himself on the darning-needle. "What sort of a feller's that?"

"I'm not a 'feller' – I'm a lady," said the darning-needle, but nobody heard her. Her sealing-wax was all gone and she'd turned black, but black makes you look so slim that she thought she was even finer than before.

"Here – there's an eggshell sailing down there," said the boys, and so they stuck the darning-needle into the shell.

"White walls – and I'm black," said the darning-needle. "How very fetching! Now they can see me – but let's hope I don't get sea-sick, then I should break!" But she didn't get sea-sick so she didn't break. "A steel stomach's a good thing for sea-sick-ness, and also the knowledge that one is rather more than an ordinary person! I do feel better! Ah, yes! – the finer one is, the more one can bear."

"Crack!"

went the eggshell,

as a wagon went over it.

"Hoo, what a squeeze!" said

the darning-needle. "Now I shall be

sea-sick! I'm breaking! I'm breaking!"

But she didn't break even though the wagon

went over her. She lay there at full length –

and there she can stay!

Grief

WHAT WE'VE GOT HERE is a story in two parts. The first part we could well do without – but it gives you the background, and that's useful.

We were staying on someone's estate out in the country and it so happened that the family were away for a few days. Along came a lady from the nearby market-town, with a little old pug-dog under her arm. She said she'd come for someone to take some shares in her tannery. She'd got her papers with her, so we advised her to put them in an envelope and direct it to the owner of the estate: "General Commissioner for War, Royal Knight," and so on.

She listened to us; she picked up a pen, she paused, and then she asked us to repeat the address, but slowly. This we did and she started to write – but in the middle of "General Commissioner..." she stopped, sighed, and said, "I'm only a woman!"

She'd sat the little old pug-dog on the floor while she was writing and he growled; after all, he'd been brought along as a treat, and for the sake of his health, and not for someone to put him on the floor. He'd got a pug-nose and looked rather fat.

"He won't bite!" said the lady, "he hasn't got any teeth. He's really like one of the family, loyal and bad-tempered, but that's because my grandchildren tease him; they play weddings and they will make him be bridesmaid and that's too much for him, the poor old chap!"

And she left her papers and put the little old pug-dog back under her arm.

That's the first part of the story – the bit
we might have done without.

The little old pug-dog died! That's the second part.

It was a week or so later. We'd come to the town and put up at an inn. Our window looked out over

80

a yard, divided up by a fence into two sections. In one of them were hanging lots of skins and hides, treated and untreated, all the paraphernalia of a tannery – the very one belonging to the widow.

The pug-dog had died that morning and was buried here in the yard; the widow's grandchildren (that's to say the tannery widow's not the pug-dog's, because he'd never married) patted down the grave – and a very nice grave it was too; it would have been a pleasure to lie in it.

The grave was bordered with broken bits of flower-pot, and covered with sand; on top of it they'd stuck half a beer-bottle with its neck poking up, but it wasn't meant to be symbolic.

The children danced round the grave and the oldest boy – a practical youth of seven years old – suggested that they should put the little old pug-dog's grave on exhibition for everyone in the street. The entrance fee was a trouser-button, something which every boy would have, and he could probably spare another one to bring in a little girl; and everyone agreed it was a jolly good idea.

*E*very time the gate opened she looked
for as long as she could.

So all the children from the street, and the back alley too, came along and paid their buttons and plenty of them went around for the rest of the afternoon with their trousers loose, but they'd seen the pug-dog's grave and that was worth it.

But outside the tanner's yard, close by the gate, there stood a little ragged girl, – so pretty, with her hair all curly, and her eyes so blue and so bright – she was a picture. She didn't say a word; she never cried, but every time the gate opened, she looked for as long as she could. She knew very well that she didn't have a button, so she stood woefully outside – stood there till everyone had had a look and everyone had gone away. Then she sat down, put her small brown hands over her eyes and burst into tears. She was the only one who hadn't seen the little pug-dog's grave. Now that was grief – and it was as great as any that we grown-ups might feel.

We saw it all from up above and, seen from above, like many of our own and other people's sorrows, it was something that seemed pretty ludicrous.

So that's the story, and if any of you don't understand it, then you can go and take some shares in the widow's tannery.

The Shepherdess and the Chimney-sweep

HAVE YOU EVER SEEN a really old wooden cupboard, all black with age and carved with scrolls and foliage? Well, a cupboard like that stood in the sitting-room.

It had come down from Great-grandma and was carved from top to bottom with roses and tulips, and amongst the most amazing scroll-work stuck out the heads of small deer with lots of antlers. In the middle of the cupboard the complete figure of a man had been cut, looking very funny, and grinning a grin that you would not care to call a laugh. He had the legs of a goat, small horns in his forehead and a long beard. The children of the house always called him

Billygoat-legs-Lieutenant-Major-General-Battle-boss,
because that was a hard name to say and there aren't
many people with a title like that – and it was quite
something to have him as a carving.

So there he was! He was always looking at the
table under the mirror, because a graceful little
china shepherdess was standing there. Her shoes
were gilded, her dress was prettily caught up with a
red rose and she had a gold bonnet and a shep-
herd's crook. She was beautiful.

Right beside her stood a little chimney-sweep,
black as coal, and, like her, made of porcelain. He
was as neat and clean as anyone else and really only
a pretend chimney-sweep. The people at the
porcelain works might just as well have made a
prince out of him for all we know.

He stood there prettily with his ladder and with
his face as pink and white as a girl's – which was
surely a mistake, for there ought to have been a
little bit of black on it somewhere. He stood very
close to the shepherdess. They'd been placed
together as a pair, and since they'd been placed like
that they were betrothed. Indeed, they were made
for each other – young people made from the same
clay and equally fragile.

*He was always looking at the table
under the mirror.*

Next door to them stood yet another figure, three times as big. He was an old Chinaman who could nod his head. He was made of porcelain too and he claimed to be the little shepherdess's grand- father, but he couldn't prove it. He maintained that he had rights over her, and so he had nodded at Billygoat- legs-Lieutenant-Major- General-Battle-boss to let him know that he could marry the little shepherdess.

"That way you'll get a man," said the old China- man. "A man who is, I fancy, mahogany all through and who will make you Mrs Billygoat-legs-Lieutenant-Major-General-Battle-boss. He has a whole cupboard full of silver-plate, as well as what he's got in secret hiding-places."

"I'm not going into that dark cupboard," said the little shepherdess. "People say he's got eleven china wives in there."

"Well, then, you can be the twelfth," said the Chinaman. "Tonight, as soon as the old cupboard creaks, you shall be married, or I'm not a Chinaman," and he nodded his head and fell fast asleep.

But the little shepherdess wept and looked across at her dearest sweetheart, the china chimney-sweep.

"I think," she said, "I must ask you to come with me out into the wide world, for I can't stay here."

"I will do anything you want," said the little chimney-sweep. "Let's go straight away. I think, with my job, that I can look after you."

"If only we were down from this table," she said. "I shan't be happy till we're out in the wide world!"

So he comforted her and showed her how she must put her little foot into the carved edges and the gilded foliage down the legs of the table. He brought his ladder, too, to help, and soon they were down on the floor. But when they looked up at the old cupboard there was a great commotion going on. All the carved deer were poking out their heads, shaking their antlers and swaying their necks about. Billygoat-legs-Lieutenant-Major-General-Battle-boss was jumping up in the air and calling across to the old Chinaman: "Now they're running away! Now they're running away!"

So they were a bit frightened, and they quickly jumped up into the drawer in the window-seat. Here, there were three or four packs of cards scattered around (none of them complete) and a little puppet-theatre which was set up as well as could be managed. A comedy was on, and all the queens – diamonds, hearts, clubs and spades – were sitting in the front row, fanning themselves with their tulips, while behind them all the knaves were standing, showing they'd got heads, top and bottom, as is the way with playing-cards. The comedy was about a couple who weren't able to get married, so the shepherdess burst into tears because it was so like her own story.

"I can't be doing with it!" she said. "I must get out of this drawer!" But when they got to the floor and looked up at the table they saw the old Chinaman was awake and swaying to and fro with his whole body, because he was just one solid lump from the neck downwards.

"Now the old Chinaman's coming!" screamed the little shepherdess, and she was so alarmed that she fell to her porcelain knees.

"I've got an idea!" said the chimney-sweep. "Why don't we sneak into the big pot-pourri pot over there in the corner? Then we shall have roses and lavender to lie on and we can throw salt in his eyes if he comes near us!"

"Now the old Chinaman's coming!"
screamed the little shepherdess.

"It wouldn't work," said the shepherdess, "and besides, I know that the old Chinaman and the potpourri pot were once engaged, and there's always a bit of fellow-feeling left between people who've been on terms like that. No! There's nothing for it but to go out into the wide, wide world."

"Will you really dare to come with me into the wide world?" asked the chimney-sweep. "Have you really thought what a big place it is, and how we'll never be able to get back here?"

"Yes, I've done that," she said.

And the chimney-sweep looked hard at her and then he said, "Chimneys are my line! Will you really dare to creep into the stove with me – first into the firebox, then into the stove-pipe? That way we can get into the chimney and I shall know what to do there. We shall climb so high that they'll never get near us, and up at the top there's a hole leading out into the wide world."

So he led her to the door of the stove.

"That looks very dirty," she said, but she still went with him. Both of them went together into the firebox, then into the stove-pipe where everything was as black as pitch.

"Now we're in the chimney," he said, "and look!

Just look up there! A beautiful star shining!"

And it really was a star shining down at them from the heavens as if it wanted to show them the way. So they crept and they crawled – it was a horrid journey – so high ... so high. But he lifted her lightly, and held her, and showed her where she should put her little porcelain feet, and that way they reached the top of the chimney-pot. There they sat down, for they were totally exhausted – as well they might be.

The sky, with all its stars, was high above them, and all the roofs of the town below. Everything spread so widely – there were such distances out in the world. The poor shepherdess never thought that such a thing could be. She laid her little head against the chimney-sweep and she cried so much that the gilt ran down off her girdle.

"It's all too much," she said. "I can't do it! The world's just too big! If only I were back again on the little table under the mirror! I shan't be happy until I'm back there again! Oh – I followed you out into the wide world, and now you must be kind enough to follow me home again if you care for me at all!"

The chimney-sweep talked to her quietly and reasonably. He talked to her about the old Chinaman and about Billygoat-legs-Lieutenant-Major-General-Battle-boss, but she sobbed so bitterly and she kissed her little chimney-sweep so, that he couldn't do anything but give way to her, even if that was stupid.

And so, with great difficulty, they crawled back down the chimney, and crept back into the stove-pipe and the firebox, (which was not at all comfortable) and there they were, back again in the gloomy old stove. They listened behind the doors to try to find out how things stood in the room. Everything was very quiet. They peeped out and – oh no! There, in the middle of the floor, lay the old Chinaman, who had fallen down off the table. He had tried to come after them, and now he lay broken in three pieces. All his back had come off in one chunk and his head had rolled into a corner.

Billygoat-legs-Lieutenant-Major-General-Battle-boss stood where he always stood, thinking things over.

"Oh, that's horrible!" said the little shepherdess.

*The old Chinaman had fallen
down off the table.*

"Dear old Grandad is broken in pieces and it's all our fault! I shall never get over it!" And she wrung her little tiny hands.

"They can still rivet him," said the chimney-sweep. "They can easily rivet him! Don't be so upset. If they glue his back together and put a rivet in the back of his head he'll be as good as new again and then he'll have a lot of nasty things to say to us."

"Do you think so?" she said, and they crept back up on to the table again where they had stood before.

"What a long way we've come," said the chimney-sweep, "and we could have saved ourselves all that trouble."

"If only we could have my old grandfather back," said the shepherdess. "Is it going to be expensive to rivet him?"

And he was riveted. The family had his back glued together, and with a tight rivet in his neck he was as good as new. But he couldn't nod any more.

"You've got very stuck-up since you went to pieces," said Billygoat-legs-Lieutenant-Major-General-Battle-boss. "I don't see that it's anything to be proud of! Shall I have her, or shan't I have her?"

And the chimney-sweep and the little shepherdess looked so touchingly at the old Chinaman.
They were so frightened he would nod his head.
But he couldn't do that any more, and it was very
embarrassing for him to explain to visitors that he
couldn't nod because the back of his neck was
permanently riveted.

So the little porcelain people were together and
they blessed the grandfather's rivet and they loved
each other till they broke to pieces.

The Browney at the Grocer's

THERE WAS A REAL, genuine student who lived in a garret and owned nothing; and there was a real, genuine grocer who lived downstairs and owned the whole house; and the browney of the house stayed with the grocer, because every Christmas Eve he'd get a bowl of porridge with a big lump of butter in it! The grocer could easily afford to give him that, so the goblin stayed on in the shop – which is all very instructive.

One evening the student came in by the back door to buy himself some cheese and candles (he hadn't got a boy to send down for them, so he went himself). He got what he wanted, paid for it, and nodded "good evening" to the grocer and the grocer's lady (she was a woman who could do more than nod – she had a tongue like a barber's strop!). The student nodded again and then stood there reading a sheet of paper that was wrapped round the cheese. It was a page torn from an old book that ought never to have been torn up at all, an old book full of poetry.

"There's more from that over there," said the grocer. "I gave an old woman some coffee beans for it. You can have the rest for fourpence."

"Thank you," said the student. "Let me swap it for the cheese – I don't need that with bread and butter! It'd be a sin for that book to be torn to pieces. You're a splendid man – a practical man – but you've as much poetry in you as that tub!"

And that was a rude thing to say – especially about the tub – but the student laughed and the grocer laughed, because it was all said as a kind of joke. It made the browney cross, though, that anyone should dare to talk like that to a grocer who lived in his own house and sold the best butter.

That same night, with the shop closed, and everyone except the student in bed, the browney went in and took the lady's stroppy tongue out of her head (she didn't really need it while she was asleep). And whenever he put it on any of the things downstairs they took on powers of speech and could say what they thought or felt about matters, just as well as the lady could herself. But only one thing could have it at a time, which was a good job, because otherwise they'd all have talked at once.

The browney put the tongue on the tub where the old newspapers were. "Is it really true," he asked, "that you don't know what poetry is?"

"Oh, I know all about that," said the tub. "It's something down the bottom of the page in the papers that gets cut out! I reckon there's more of it in me than there is in that student, and I'm only a poor tub alongside the grocer!"

And the goblin put the tongue on the coffee-mill – goodness, how it went! – and he put it on the butter-cask and the till. They were all of the same opinion as the tub, and (as you know) what most people agree about has got to be respected.

"Now let's see about the student!" – and the browney went very quietly up the staircase to the garret where the student lived. The candle was

101

burning there and the browney peeped through the keyhole and saw the student reading the battered old book from downstairs. But how bright it was in there! Out of the book came a clear shaft of light, growing into a trunk – into a huge tree which lifted up its branches and spread them out over the student. Every leaf glinted and every blossom was the delicate head of a girl; some had dark, glistening eyes, others had blue ones – wonderfully clear. Every fruit was a shining star that seemed to be singing and ringing with melody.

Never had the little browney imagined such glory, let alone seen or heard it. And so he stood there on tiptoe, peeping and peeping till the light went out. The student must have blown out the candle and gone to bed, but the little browney still went on standing there, for the singing went on, softly and delicately; it was a beautiful cradle song for the tired student.

"How splendid it is here!" said the little browney, "I must say I didn't bargain for this! I fancy I'd like to stay here with the student!" and he thought – and he thought wisely – and then he sighed: "The student hasn't got any porridge!" So he went – yes – he went back down to the grocer's; and not a minute

*Never had the little browney
imagined such glory.*

too soon, either, for the tub had almost worn out the old lady's tongue by talking about what was inside him first from one point of view and then turning it round to talk about it from another.

So the browney came and took the tongue back to the lady. But from that time on the whole shop, from the till to the firewood, took its opinions from the tub and held him in such high esteem, and thought so much of him, that whenever the grocer read out the art and theatre columns in the newspaper they thought it all came from the tub.

But the little browney couldn't sit quietly downstairs any more, listening to all that wise and learned talk, for as soon as the light shone from the garret, it was as though its beams were strong cables drawing him up and he had to go and peep through the keyhole; then there surged over him the sort of greatness you feel down by the thundering sea when the god of storms sweeps over it, and he would burst into tears. He didn't know himself what he was crying for, but there was a kind of blessing in those tears! How marvellous it would be to sit with the student under that tree, but that was impossible – he had to make do with the keyhole. So there he stood, on the cold landing, with the autumn wind blowing down on him from the trap-door into the loft, and it was cold – so cold – but the little fellow only noticed that when the light went out and the music died away on the wind. Hoo! He was frozen – and he crept downstairs again into his warm corner where everything was cosy and comfortable. And then the Christmas porridge would come with the big lump of butter – oh, yes, the grocer was the one who mattered!

But late one night the browney was woken by a terrible banging on the window-shutters. People outside were thumping on them, and the night watchman was blowing his whistle. There was a great fire – the whole street was lit up by flames. Was it here in this house or next door? Where? Everyone panicked! The grocer's lady was so flustered that she took her gold earrings out of her ears and put them in her pocket to be sure of saving something. The grocer ran for his share certificates, and the maid for the silk mantilla that she'd been able to buy. Everybody wanted to save his treasures – the little browney, too – and with a few big leaps he was up the stairs

The greatest treasure in the
house was saved!

and in beside the student where he stood quietly at the open window looking at the fire in a house across the road. The little browney grabbed the wonderful book from the table, stuck it into his red hood and held it there with both hands – the greatest treasure in the house was saved! And so he fled up, and on to the roof, right up by the chimney-pot, and there he sat all lit up by the burning house opposite, holding on with both hands to his red hood with the treasure in it.

Now he knew where his heart was and where he really belonged; but when the fire was out and he stopped to think – yes! – "I'll split myself between them," he said. "I can't give up the grocer because of the porridge!"

And that was very human of him!

We all of us go to the grocer –

for the porridge.

∞

The Snowman

"I'M ALL OF A CRACKLE inside with this delicious cold!" said the snowman. "The wind really blows a bit of life into you! And how that glowing thing glowers!" (He meant the sun, which was now about to set.) "He'll not make me blink. I can still keep hold of my bits and pieces."

He was talking about two big triangular bits of tile which were his eyes; his mouth was part of an old rake, so he had teeth too. He'd been born to the sound of boys cheering and greeted with the jingle of sleigh-bells and the cracking of whips.

The sun set. The full moon came up, big and round, shining white and beautiful in the darkening air. "Here he comes again from the other side," said the snowman. (He thought it was the sun come up again.) "I saw him off with all his glowering! Now he can hang up there and shine away so that I can see myself. If only I knew how people moved and got about! I'd very much like to get about myself! If I could, I'd go down there and slide on the ice like I saw the boys doing, but I don't know how to run."

"Grroff! Grroff!" barked the old watchdog. He was a bit hoarse, and that was since the days when he'd been a house-dog and lain by the fire. "The sun'll teach you how to run! I saw that with the chap who was here before you – and with the chap before him. Grroff! Grroff! Everybody grroff!"

"Now then, friend, I don't know what you're talking about!" said the snowman. "Him up there teach me to run?" (He meant the moon.) "Oh, yes! He was running himself right enough last time I looked at him; now he's sneaking back from the other side."

"You're stupid," said the watchdog, "but then you've only just been slapped together! What you're looking at now is called the moon; the sun was the one before. He'll come again tomorrow morning and he'll teach you to run down there into

"*You're stupid,*" said the watchdog,

"*but then you've only just been slapped together.*"

the ditch by the wall. We're in for a change of weather – I can tell because I get pains in my left back leg. We're in for a shift in the weather."

"I don't know what he's talking about at all," said the snowman, "but I've an idea that it's not something nice. That thing that glowered and then disappeared, the thing he called the sun, is certainly no friend of mine – I can feel it in my bones."

"Grroff! Grroff!" barked the watchdog. He turned round three times and lay down in the kennel to go to sleep.

And a change in the weather did come. Towards morning there was a thick, clammy mist over everything; then later the wind got up – icy cold – and the frost gripped everything. But what a sight it was when the sun came up! All the trees and bushes were covered with hoar-frost, like a whole forest of white coral, where all the twigs bloomed with glittering white flames. The delicate tracery of branches, which you can't see in summer because of all the leaves, now showed up clearly. It was like lace, gleaming white, with white lights glimmering from every twig. The birch tree lifted its branches to the wind, live, like the trees in summer; it was wonderfully beautiful! And when the sun shone down, everything sparkled as if it were powdered with a dust of diamonds, with big diamonds glinting in the drifts of snow. You'd think that countless little lights were burning, whiter than the white snow.

"That is wonderfully beautiful," said a young girl, coming out into the garden with a young man and standing next to the snowman, looking at the glittering trees. "You wouldn't see it so beautiful, even in summer!" she said, and her eyes sparkled.

"And you won't have a fellow like this here then," said the young man, and he pointed to the snowman. "He's splendid."

The young girl laughed, nodded at the snowman and danced off with her friend over the snow, which crunched under her as though she was walking on starch.

"Who were those two?" the snowman asked the watchdog. "You've been on this farm longer than I have. Do you know 'em?"

"Of course I do!" said the watchdog. "She's patted me and he's given me bones. I don't bite them."

"But what are they up to here?" asked the snowman.

"Courrrr– courrrr– courting!" said the watchdog. "They'll be moving into the same kennel and gnawing bones together. Grroff! Grroff!"

"And are those two as important as you and me?" asked the snowman.

"They belong to the guvnor," said the watchdog. "Really, people born yesterday are an ignorant lot, and you're one of 'em! As for me – I'm old and wise; I know everything that's going on at this farm. And what's more, I remember a time when I wasn't chained up out here in the cold. Grroff! Grroff!"

"The cold's very nice," said the snowman. "But come on, tell me all about it – only don't keep rattling your chain, it gives me the shivers inside."

"Grroff! Grroff!" barked the watchdog. "I was young once. 'Oh, isn't he a sweet little thing,' they used to say, and I lay in a velvet chair up there in the farmhouse, lay in the guvnor's lap. They used to kiss my nose and wipe my paws with an embroidered handkerchief and it was all 'prettykins' and 'dear little doggy'. But then I got too big for them, so they gave me to the housekeeper and I

114

"*I was young once,*" *said the watchdog.*

"*And I lay in a velvet chair.*"

had to live in the basement! You can see where it was from where you're standing; you can see down into the room where I was guvnor – because that's what I was at the house-keeper's. It may have been a smaller place than upstairs, but I was more comfortable, and I wasn't pulled around and slobbered over by the children like upstairs. The food was just as good as before, and there was more of it! I had my own cushion, and there was a stove that was the best place in the world at times like this! I used to creep down under it so that I got black all over. Oh – I still dream about that stove. Grroff! Grroff!"

"Does a stove look as nice as all that?" asked the snowman. "Like me?"

"Like the opposite of you! It's coal-black, it's got a long neck with a brass collar, and it eats firewood so that flames come out of its mouth. If you get down beside it or, better still, under it, then it's the most comfortable place in the world! You can see it through the window from where you're standing!"

And the snowman looked, and sure enough he saw a black, polished thing with a brass collar and flames flickering down below. The snowman came over all peculiar. He had a strange feeling that he couldn't put a name to; it wasn't anything he knew about – but most people will know it, provided they're not snowmen.

"And why did you leave her?" asked the snowman. (He felt that the stove must be some kind of woman.) "How could you leave such a lovely place?"

"I'd no choice," said the watchdog. "They threw me out and chained me up here. I'd bitten the youngest master in the leg because he pinched the bone that I was gnawing. Well – 'bone for bone,' says I, but they didn't like it, and since then I've been on this chain, and I've lost my nice voice. Just hear how hoarse I am: Grroff! Grroff! That's the end of it."

But the snowman wasn't listening; he kept on looking into the housekeeper's room where the stove stood on its four iron legs, the same height as the snowman himself.

"Everything's scrunching down inside me," he said. "Shall I ever get in there? It's an innocent enough wish, and innocent wishes must surely be granted. It's my highest wish, my very only wish, and it really wouldn't be fair for it not to be granted. I must get in there, I must get beside her, even if I have to break a window."

"You'll never get in," said the watchdog, "and if you did reach the stove then you'd soon get off – Grroff! Grroff!"

"I'm as good as off," said the snowman. "I think I'm breaking up."

The snowman stood there for the whole day, looking through the window. As the light faded, the room looked even more inviting. A gentle light came from the stove, not like the moon or the sun – no, it was ... like a stove when it's got something inside it! When they opened its door, flames leapt out as they always did. It made the snowman's white face red with blushes which went on half-way down his body.

"I can't take it," he said. "How beautiful she is with her tongue out!"

It was a long, long night – but not for the snowman. He was lost in his own beautiful thoughts and freezing till he crackled.

In the morning, the basement windows were frozen over with the most beautiful flowers of ice that any snowman could wish for – but they hid the

*It was a long, long night – but
not for the snowman.*

stove. The ice wouldn't melt on the panes, so he couldn't see her. Everything crackled and crunched; it was just the kind of frosty weather that a snowman should enjoy – but he didn't enjoy it. He could – and really should – have felt so light-hearted, but he wasn't light-hearted. He was love-sick for the stove.

"That's a nasty complaint for a snowman," said the watchdog. "Mind you, I've had it myself, but I got over it. Grroff! Grroff! Now we'll get a shift in the weather."

And the weather did shift; it began to thaw. And the more the weather thawed, the more the snow-man thawed too. But he didn't say anything, he didn't grizzle – and that's a sure sign…

One morning he collapsed. Where he had stood something stuck up in the air like the handle of a broom, and that's what the boys had built him round.

"Now I can see why he was love-sick," said the watchdog. "The snow-man had a stove-rake in his body, and that's what was making him spooney – but now he's got over it. Grroff! Grroff!"

And soon they all got over the weather too.

"Grroff! Grroff!" barked the watchdog – but the little girls on the farm sang:

> *"Primrose, primrose*
> *Pretty face!*
> *Willow, willow*
> *Woolly lace!*
> *Lark and cuckoo*
> *Come and sing,*
> *February*
> *Heralds spring.*
> *Whistle, whistle*
> *Call – call –*
> *Come the sunshine*
> *Over all."*

And nobody thought about the snowman.

The Fir Tree

OUT IN THE FOREST was a pretty little fir tree. It stood in a nice, airy spot, where the sun could get at it, and it had lots of bigger companions growing round it – pines, as well as firs. But the little fir tree was in a great hurry to grow up: it thought nothing of the warm sunshine and the fresh air; it didn't give the village children a second look when they went chattering along, looking for wild strawberries and raspberries. Sometimes they'd come with a whole crock full, or they'd have strawberries actually threaded on a straw, and they'd sit down by the little tree and say: "Oh – isn't that a dainty little one!" But the little tree didn't like to hear that sort of thing at all.

The next year it was bigger by a good stretch, and the year after that it was taller still – and you'd see that by its rings, because fir trees have one for every year they grow.

"Oh, if only I were a great big tree like those others!" sighed the little tree. "Then I'd spread my branches out wide and I'd look out from my top over all the wide world! The birds would build nests in my branches, and when the wind blew I'd nod as gracefully as those others over there!" It took no pleasure in the sunshine and the birds, or in the rosy clouds that drifted over it, morning and evening.

And when winter came and the snow lay glittering white all around, a hare might come bounding along and jump right over the little tree – that was annoying! But two winters passed and when the third came the tree was so big that hares now had to go round it. Oh, to grow, to grow, to get big and old – that was surely the only pleasure in the whole world, thought the tree.

In the autumn, the woodcutters used to come and cut down some of the largest trees. It happened every year and the young fir tree (who was now growing up very nicely)

shuddered as the tall, splendid trees fell tearing and crashing to the ground. Their branches were lopped off so that they looked long and thin and bare – you'd hardly recognize them – and they were loaded on to wagons, and horses pulled them off out of the forest.

Where were they going to, then? What would happen to them?

In the spring, when the swallows came, and the storks, the tree asked them, "Do you know where they were taken? Didn't you meet them?"

The swallows didn't know anything about it, but a stork looked wise and nodded his head and said, "Oh, yes; I think I know that. I met up with a lot of new ships when I was flying here from Egypt, and these ships had some splendid tall masts and I fancy that'd be them – they smelt like fir. I must say they did you proud – very smart, they were, very smart!"

"Oh, how I wish that I were big enough to set off over the sea like that. But what's the sea really like? How does it look?"

"Dear me," said the stork. "That's far too complicated to explain," and he went away.

"Enjoy yourself while you're young," said the sunbeams. "Enjoy yourself while you're growing up, with all that life in you!" And the wind brushed the tree with kisses and the dew covered it with tears, but the fir tree just didn't know what they were up to.

When it was nearly Christmas some quite young trees were cut down – some of them neither so big nor so old as our fidgety fir tree, with all its need to be up and doing. These young trees (and they were altogether the most beautiful ones) kept all their branches when they were loaded on to the wagons and when the horses pulled them off out of the forest.

"Where are they going to?" asked the fir tree. "They're no bigger than me – in fact there was one who was a lot smaller. Why do they keep all their branches? Where are they taken to?"

"We see it! We see it!" twittered the sparrows. "We've been peeking in at the windows down in the town! We know where they're taken to! Ooh, they get as rich and splendid as you can imagine! We've peeked in the windows and seen how they're planted in the middle of warm rooms and decorated with the most beautiful things – golden apples, honey-cakes, toys and hundreds of candles!"

"And then?" asked the fir tree, trembling through all its branches. "And then? What happens then?"

"Where are they taken to?"
asked the fir tree.

"Oh, we've not seen more than that! But that was beyond anything!"

"Then maybe I'll be bound for a splendid trip like that one day?" said the tree, full of joy. "That'll be even better than going over the sea! Oh, how I ache with longing! If only it were Christmas! I'm as tall now and as branchy as the others who were taken last year! Oh, that I were up on that wagon – or in that warm room with all the pomp and splendour! And then – ? Oh, yes, something even better will happen, even more beautiful, else why should they decorate me? Something must happen that's even bigger, even better – ! But what? Oh, how I ache! How I long for it all! I don't for the life of me know what's come over me!"

"Enjoy yourself with me!" said the air and the sunshine. "Enjoy being young outside in the open air!"

But the fir tree didn't enjoy such things in the least. It grew and it grew. Winter and summer it stood there, all green. All dark green it stood there, and people who saw it said, "What a lovely tree!" So when Christmas came it was the first one of all to be cut down.

The axe cut deep into its pith; the tree fell to

earth with a sigh; it felt a pain, a faintness; it couldn't think about being happy; it was saddened to be leaving its home, its place, where it had its roots. Now it knew that it would never again see its dear old friends, the little shrubs and flowers round about – perhaps not even the birds. No joy in a parting like that.

The tree only came to its senses when it was unloaded in a yard with the other trees and it heard a man say, "That's a beauty! We don't need any but that!" So a couple of servants in full livery came along and brought the fir tree into a big, handsome room. Portraits were hanging all round on the walls, and by the big tiled stove stood big Chinese vases with lions on their lids; there were rocking-chairs there, sofas uphol-stered in silk, big tables covered with picture-books and toys worth a hundred times a hundred pounds – or that's what the children said. And the fir tree was set up in a big tub filled with sand, but you couldn't see that it was a tub because they hung it round with green baize and it stood on a broad, many-coloured carpet. Oh, how the tree trembled! What was going to happen now? The servants and the young ladies of the house came and decorated it. On one branch they hung little nets cut from coloured paper and every net was filled with sweets. Golden apples and walnuts hung down as if they grew there, and more than a hundred red, blue and white candles were fastened among the branches. Dolls which looked like real people (the tree had never seen such things before) swung among the pine needles, while right up at the top there was a big star made of golden tinsel. It was all marvellous, unspeakably marvellous.

"This evening," said everybody; "it'll really sparkle this evening."

Oh! thought the tree, if only it were evening! If only the candles were lit – and what will happen then? Perhaps the trees will come out of the forest to see me? Perhaps the sparrows will fly to the window-panes? Perhaps I shall stay growing here and keep my decorations summer and winter alike?

Oh, yes, the fir tree knew what was going on; but it got a real bark-ache from all this longing, and a bark-ache for a tree is as unpleasant as a head-ache for the rest of us.

And now the candles were lit. Such brilliance! Such splendour! The tree trembled through all its

*They hung little nets cut from coloured paper
and every net was filled with sweets.*

branches – so much so that one of the candles set fire to its needles – very painful. "Lord save us!" cried the young ladies and they put the fire out.

Now the tree didn't dare tremble – oh, that was horrible! It was so afraid of losing any of its decorations; it was altogether dazed by all the brilliance – and now the double-doors were opened and a whole crowd of children rushed in as if they wanted to up-end the whole tree. Their elders followed a bit more sedately; then the little ones stood quite still – but only for a moment, before they shouted till the room rang, and danced around the tree, and one present after another was taken down from it.

What are they doing now? thought the tree. What's going to happen? And the candles burnt down to the branches and after they'd done that somebody put them out and the children were allowed to plunder the tree. Oh, how they plunged in to do that; so that all its branches groaned and if it hadn't been fixed to the ceiling by the tip, where the gold star was, it would have toppled over.

The children danced round with all their lovely toys and nobody bothered about the tree except for an old nursemaid who came and peered in among

the branches – but that was only to see if anyone had missed a fig or an apple.

"A story, a story!" shouted the children and pulled a little fat man over to the tree, and he sat down right beneath it.

"Just as if we were in the greenwood," he said, "and the tree can have the singular good fortune to hear it as well! But I'm only going to tell one story. Do you want the one about Henny Penny or the one about Klumpa Dumpa, who fell downstairs but still rose up to be the highest in the land and married the princess?"

"Henny Penny!" cried some; "Klumpa Dumpa!" cried others; and there was a lot of yelling and shouting. Only the fir tree stayed quite still, thinking, Shall I be in it? Shall I have something to do? But it had been in it; it had done what it was meant to do.

And the man told the story of Klumpa Dumpa, who fell downstairs but still rose up to be the highest in the land and married the princess. And the children clapped their hands and shouted, "Tell it again! Tell it again!" and

133

they wanted to have Henny Penny as well, but they only got Klumpa Dumpa. The fir tree stood there quietly and full of its own thoughts – the birds out in the forest had never told a story like that.

"Klumpa Dumpa fell downstairs, but still got the princess." Ah, yes! Ah, yes! Such things can happen in the world, thought the fir tree, and believed it all true because it was such a nice man who told it. Ah, yes, ah, yes, who knows? Perhaps I'll fall downstairs too and marry a princess! And it looked forward happily to the next day when it would be decorated with candles and toys, and gold and fruit.

I won't shiver and shake tomorrow, it thought, I'll really enjoy being so splendid. And what's more, I'll be able to hear the story of Klumpa Dumpa again tomorrow, and perhaps Henny Penny as well. And the tree stood quiet and thoughtful the whole night long. Next morning in came the men and the housemaids.

Now we're back to decorating, thought the tree, but they dragged it out of the room, up the staircase, into the loft, and there they stowed it, in a dark corner, away from any chink of daylight. What's the meaning of this? thought the tree. What do you

The tree stood quiet and thoughtful
the whole night long.

think I'm to do here? What do you think I'll listen to here? And it leaned up against the wall and stood there, thinking and thinking. It had plenty of time for this as the days and nights went by. Nobody came up there, and, although someone did come eventually, it was only to stow some big tea-chests in the corner. The tree was quite hidden, and you'd think it was totally forgotten.

It's winter out there now! thought the tree. The earth's hard and covered with snow; the people can't take me out and plant me so I suppose I'm to shelter here till the spring. That's a kindly thought; how very kind these people are! If only it weren't so dark here and so horribly lonely! Not even a little hare! Oh, it was so nice out in the forest with the snow on the ground and the hare jumping past – yes, even when he jumped over me, although I didn't like it at the time. But up here it's horribly lonely!

"Peep! peep!" said a little mouse just at that moment, and crept forward, and another little one followed. They sniffed at the fir tree and crept in among its branches.

"It's beastly cold," said the little mice. "Otherwise this would be a fine place to be. Don't you think so, you old tree?"

"Not so much of the 'old'," said the fir tree. "There's plenty older than me."

"Where are you from?" asked the mice. "And what sort of things do you know about?" (They were really dreadfully inquisitive.) "Tell us, what's the most beautiful place on earth? Have you ever been there? Have you ever been down in the larder, where there's cheeses lying on the shelves and hams hanging from the ceiling, where you can dance on the tallow candles, and go in thin and come out fat?"

"I don't know anything about that," said the tree, "but I do know about the forest, where the sun shines and the birds sing." And it told them all about its early days, and the little mice had never heard anything like that before and they listened, and listened, and then they said, "Cor, what a lot you've seen! How happy you must've been!"

"Me?" said the fir tree, and it thought about everything it had said. "Yes, on the whole those were pretty good times!" But then it told them about that Christmas Eve when it was hung with sweets and candles.

"Ooh!" said the little mice. "How lucky you were, you old fir tree!"

"Not so much of the 'old'!" said the tree. "It was just this winter that I came out of the forest; I'm absolutely in my prime; it's only that I'm not growing at the moment."

"What beautiful stories you tell!" said the little mice, and the next night they came with four more little mice to listen to the tree, and the more it told them, the more clearly it remembered everything and it thought, Yes, those were pretty good times – but they can come again yet, they can come again! Klumpa Dumpa fell downstairs and still married the princess. Perhaps I'll marry a princess, too!

And then the fir tree thought of a pretty little birch tree that grew out there in the forest, and to the fir tree the birch really seemed like a beautiful princess.

"Who's Klumpa Dumpa?" asked the little mice. So the fir tree told them the whole story, remembering every single word; and the little mice were ready to jump up to the top of the tree for pure pleasure. And the next night a great many more mice came along, and on Sunday even a couple of rats; but they said the story wasn't much good, and that made the little mice sorry, so that now it didn't seem so good to them either.

"Is that the only story you know?" asked the rats.

"The only one," answered the tree. "I heard it on the happiest night of my life – although at the time I didn't really think how happy I was."

"It's a remarkably dull story! Don't you know one about bacon or tallow-candles? A larder tale?"

"No," said the tree.

"Well, thanks very much for that!" said the rats and they went back to where they came from.

Eventually, the little mice stayed away too, and the tree sighed, "Oh, it was lovely when they all sat round me, those jolly little mice, and listened to what I had to tell. Now that's over and done with too! But I'll remember to make the most of things when they take me out again!"

And when did that happen? Well, it was one morning – a lot of people came and rummaged around in the attic. Packing cases were put away and the tree pulled out. It's true they shoved it rather roughly over the floor, but a servant dragged it straight away to the stairs and the daylight.

Now life starts all over again! thought the tree as

it felt the freshness of the air, the first rays of the sun – and now it was out in the yard. Everything happened so quickly that the tree forgot to take a look at itself; there was so much to see all around. The yard was next to a garden where everything was in bloom: the roses hung fresh and fragrant over a little trellis, the lindens were in flower and swallows flew about crying, "Kvirre-virre-veet, my old man's back," but they weren't talking about the fir tree.

"Now I'm coming back to life!" it chortled, and stretched wide its branches – but aah! they were all withered and yellow. It lay in a corner among the weeds and nettles. The gold tinsel star was still fixed to its top and it glittered in the bright sunshine.

In the yard itself a few of the jolly children were playing – the ones who had danced round the tree at Christmas-time and enjoyed themselves so much. One of the youngest ran up and pulled off the golden star.

"See what's still sticking to that mucky old Christmas tree!" he said, and stamped on its branches so that they cracked under his boots.

And the tree looked at the fresh garden in all its coloured splendour, and then it looked at itself and wished that it had stayed behind in its dark corner of the loft. It thought about its brisk early days in the forest, about that cheerful Christmas Eve and about the little mice who had so much enjoyed listening to the story of Klumpa Dumpa.

"It's all gone! All gone!" said the poor tree. "I should have enjoyed myself when I could. All gone! All gone!"

And the servant came and chopped the tree into small pieces, a whole bundle of them. It made a fine blaze under the big wash-tub, and it sighed deeply so that every sigh was like a little pistol-shot. This drew the boys over who were playing there, and they sat round the fire, looked into it and shouted, "Piff! Paff!". But with every puffing noise that was like a deep sigh the tree thought of a summer's day in the forest, a winter's night out there under the glittering stars. It thought about Christmas Eve and Klumpa Dumpa, the only story it had ever heard or knew how to tell – and so the tree was burnt up. The boys played in the yard, and the smallest one had on his chest the gold star which the tree had worn on the happiest evening of its life.

Now that was gone, and the tree was gone, and the story too: all gone, all gone – and that's the way with all the stories...

SOME WORDS FROM THE MOLE

I don't see too good, you know, but whoever made these stories had a pretty sharp eye. You can tell from the way he talks about everyone that he could see further into a block of wood than most of us. A few words though I didn't quite follow, so I burrowed around and here are a few things I dug up…

Ducks-and-drakes (page 13)
What some people call that game where you skim flat stones over water.

Tinder-box (page 18)
An ancient kind of lighter: bits of dry wood in a box which you can use to get a flame by striking sparks from flint with steel.

Portents (page 24)
Signs that big things are about to happen – not necessarily good ones either: black clouds may be portents of big thunder.

Snuff-box (page 28)
A box for keeping snuff in – well – that's obvious! But snuff's funny stuff: tobacco powder which you sniff in little pinches and which needs to be kept in a tight little box or everyone will be sneezing.

Slate-pencil (page 29)
Before they had pencils and paper or computers in school, children used to write on hard black slate with a piece of softer slate, rather like chalk on a blackboard.

142

Bloodstock (page 41)
Great racehorses whose ancestors were also great racehorses.

Spittoon (page 43)
A while back, people used to spit all over the place and nobody seemed to mind; but if you wanted to do so indoors then it would be polite to use a spittoon, which was a pot specially designed for the job.

Rivet (page 43)
A metal clip used to repair broken china; here it's fitted on a doll; later (page 96) one turns up on the neck of the shepherdess's grandfather.

Jumping-jack (page 47)
A weird contraption made by stringing a slat of wood between the ends of a wishbone. Then you wind the wood up tight, let go and, with luck, it will jump around like a fire-cracker. See the picture on page 49.

Foreign legion (page 51)
A part of the French army stationed in North Africa. If you got into trouble, you could join it with no questions asked.

Morocco leather (page 53)
Expensive leather first made in Morocco from goatskins.

Boot-jack (page 61)
A device to help you pull off long riding-boots.

Prima ballerina (page 64)
A top-class lady ballet dancer.

Darning-needle (page 69)
A big needle used for mending holes in woolly socks and suchlike – very different from a delicate little sewing-needle.

Tannery (page 79)
A very smelly workshop where animal skins were treated to turn them into leather.

Pot-pourri (page 90)
A bowl or pretty jar full of dried rose petals. It gives off a musky scent, especially when the petals are mixed with lavender and a bit of brandy. You put salt in too, to preserve the mixture, and that's what the chimney-sweep was going to throw at the Chinaman.

Browney (page 99)
An unreliable household sprite; he can be helpful, but mind how you treat him.

Strop (page 100)
A strip of thick leather for sharpening up the edge of a barber's razor.

Mantilla (page 105)
I always thought this was a little cape, or cloak, but usually it's a big lacy veil which ladies (especially Spanish ones) wear over their heads and shoulders.

Baize (page 129)
Soft green felt, like the stuff they put on billiard tables.

ACKNOWLEDGEMENTS

These translations have been made from the three-volume edition of Andersen's *Samlede Eventyr og Historier* (1973) based upon the edition by Hans Brix and Anker Jensen. Some first appeared in new editions of Andrew Lang's Colour Fairy Books that were edited by the translator: "The Steadfast Tin-soldier" and "The Darning-needle" in *The Yellow Fairy Book* (1980); and "The Flying Trunk", "The Collar", "The Browney at the Grocer's", "The Snowman" and "The Fir Tree" in *The Pink Fairy Book* (1982). "Grief" was translated and told at the 18th Congress of the International Board on Books for Youth at Cambridge in 1982, and printed in their proceedings, *Story in the Child's Changing World*. "Jumpers" was translated as a contribution to a manuscript *Festschrift* for Vibeke Stybe of the Danish Children's Books Institute.